Parent's Introduction

We Both Read is the first series of books designed to invite parents and children to share the reading of a story by taking turns reading aloud. This "shared reading" innovation, which was developed with reading education specialists, invites parents to read the more complex text and storyline on the left-hand pages. Children are encouraged to read the right-hand pages, which feature less complex text and storyline, specifically written for the beginning reader. You will note that a "talking parent" icon ⬚ precedes the parent's text and a "talking child" icon ⬚ precedes the child's text.

Reading aloud is one of the most important activities parents can share with their child to assist them in their reading development. However, *We Both Read* goes beyond reading *to* a child and allows parents to share the reading *with* a child. *We Both Read* is so powerful and effective because it combines two key elements in learning: "modeling" (the parent reads) and "doing" (the child reads). The result is not only faster reading development for the child, but a much more enjoyable and enriching experience for both!

You may find it helpful to read the entire book aloud yourself the first time, then invite your child to participate in the second reading. We encourage you to share and interact with your child as you read the book together. If your child is having difficulty, you might want to mention a few things to help them. "Sounding out" is good, but it will not work with all words. They can pick up clues about the words they are reading from the story, the context of the sentence, or even the pictures. Some stories have rhyming patterns that might help. For beginning readers, you also might want to suggest touching the words with their finger as they read, so they can better connect the voice sound and the printed word.

Sharing the *We Both Read* books together will engage you and your child in an interactive adventure in reading! It is a fun and easy way to encourage and help your child to read—and a wonderful way to start them off on a lifetime of reading enjoyment!

We Both Read: My Town

———————————————

Text Copyright © 2007 by Sindy McKay
Illustrations Copyright ©2007 Meredith Johnson
All rights reserved

We Both Read® is a trademark of Treasure Bay, Inc.

Published by Treasure Bay, Inc.
40 Sir Francis Drake Boulevard
San Anselmo, CA 94960 USA

PRINTED IN SINGAPORE

Library of Congress Catalog Card Number: 2006907939

Hardcover ISBN-10: 1-60115-001-6
Hardcover ISBN-13: 978-1-60115-001-1
Paperback ISBN-10: 1-60115-002-4
Paperback ISBN-13: 978-1-60115-002-8

We Both Read® Books
Patent No. 5,957,693

Visit us online at:
www.webothread.com

WE BOTH READ®

My Town

By Sindy McKay

Illustrated by Meredith Johnson

TREASURE BAY

My dad and I like to go driving around.

He wants me to know where things are in my . . .

. . . town.

We're drawing a map of my town that's so neat!

It shows where my house is. It shows my whole . . .

. . . street.

I live near the corner of Third Street and Drew.

My address is one hundred seventy . . .

. . . two.

Now just up the street lives my best friend, Dan Coop. I mark where he lives with a basketball . . .

. . . hoop.

We go to a school that's near Second and Hop.

The sign on the corner is red and reads . . .

. . . STOP.

Turn *right* at the sign then the street takes a jag.

The school is right there. You can see a big . . .

. . . flag.

Now if you turn *left* at the corner instead, you'll come to the market where you can buy . . .

. . . bread.

Our map tells me where the police stations are. I've marked every one with a gold colored . . .

. . . star.

The firehouse sits up on Sycamore Street.
I sat in the truck once, right in the front . . .

. . . seat.

The hospital sits on a hill by a farm.

It's where my dad took me when I broke . . .

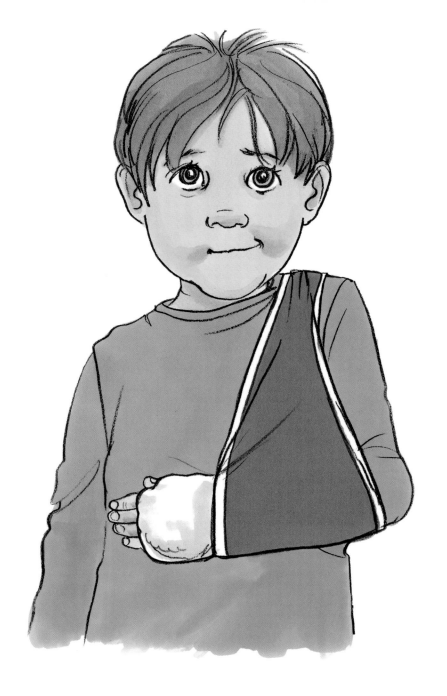

. . . my arm.

Now finding the library isn't that hard.
I walk there with Mom, but I use my own . . .

. . . card.

My dad and I work on this map as a team.
The blue color means there's a river or . . .

. . . stream.

Our map shows the west and the east side of town. The north side **is** up and the south side . . .

. . . **is** down.

My dad says we're going to "Stickles and Stones."
They have just the biggest and best . . .

. . . ice cream cones.

We walk out the door and I put on my cap.

To help find the way I have made a small . . .

. . . map.

On Drew, we head east going straight to the light.
From there, do we turn to the left or . . .

. . . the right?

We'll turn to the left onto Dickenson Street. Go north past the shoe store. I marked that with . .

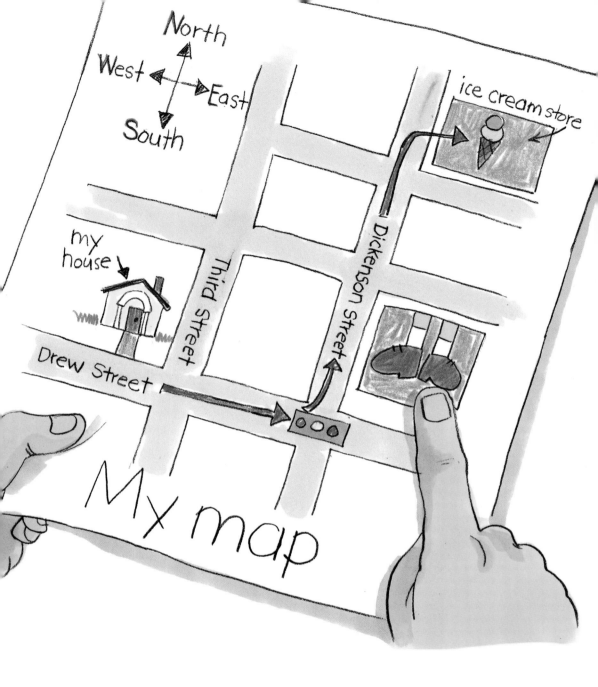

. . . feet.

We count two blocks more then we finally stop.
I'm ordering chocolate with sprinkles on . . .

. . . top.

To find any place in my town is a snap!
We just plan **our** route there by using . . .

. . . **our** map!

The End

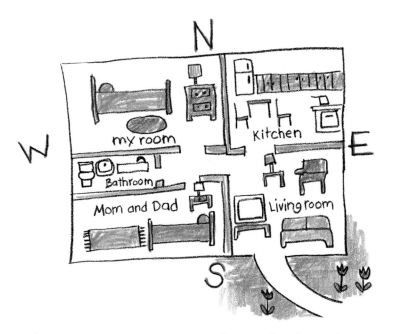

In this story, a boy and his father have a great time working together to draw a map of all the important places in their town. You can have fun drawing maps too! Here are some ideas to help you get started.

Start by first drawing a map of your house. Once you are familiar with the way a map works, you can try making a map of your neighborhood. Be sure you include your own address and the names of the streets that are around you. You can also make a map that shows how to get to a place near your house that you like to go to.

The boy in this story used a cone to show where his favorite ice cream shop is located and a basketball hoop to show where his best friend lives. You can make up your own symbols for the places that are special to you.

SOME OTHER FUN MAP ACTIVITIES

Ask an adult to make a treasure map and see if you can follow the directions to the treasure. You can even make your own treasure map!

The next time your family takes a trip, help your mom or dad map out the route you will take to your destination.

If you have access to a computer, your parents or teacher might be able to help you use the Internet to go to a site, such as Mapquest (www.mapquest.com), where you can create a map with directions from your house to a favorite location.

If you liked *My Town*, here are two other
We Both Read® Books you are sure to enjoy!

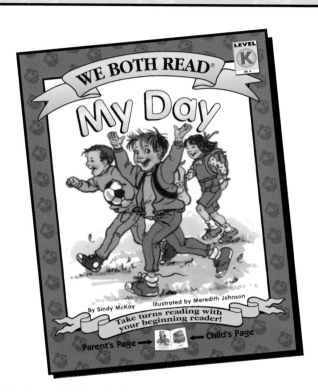

This Level K book is designed for the child who is just being introduced to reading. The child's pages have only one or two words, which relate directly to the illustration and even rhyme with what has just been read to them. This title is a charming story about what a child does in the course of a simple happy day.

To see all the We Both Read books that are available, just go online to **www.webothread.com**

This is a perfect book to encourage even pre-readers to try reading. The rhyming patterns in the story, as well as the simple words and pictures on the child's pages, make it easy for children to participate in the reading. The simple, but delightful, story is about a young boy's trip with his parents to visit his grandfather, who owns a small general store out in the countryside.